BERNARD ASHLEY

Dinner Ladies Don't Count

Illustrated by Janet Duchesne

PUFFIN BOOKS

PUFFIN BOOKS

Published by the Penguin Group
27 Wrights Lane, London w8 5TZ, England
Viking Penguin Inc., 40 West 23rd Street, New York, New York 10010, USA
Penguin Books Australia Ltd, Ringwood, Victoria, Australia
Penguin Books Canada Ltd, 2801 John Street, Markham, Ontario, Canada L3R 1B4
Penguin Books (NZ) Ltd, 182–190 Wairau Road, Auckland 10, New Zealand

Penguin Books Ltd, Registered Offices: Harmondsworth, Middlesex, England

Dinner Ladies Don't Count first published by Julia MacRae Books 1981
Linda's Lie first published by Julia MacRae Books 1982
Published in Puffin Books 1984
10 9 8

Dinner Ladies Don't Count text copyright © Bernard Ashley, 1981, illustrations
copyright © Janet Duchesne, 1981; *Linda's Lie* text copyright © Bernard Ashley,
1982, illustrations copyright © Janet Duchesne, 1982.
All rights reserved

Made and printed in Great Britain by
Richard Clay Ltd, Bungay, Suffolk
Filmset in Monophoto Baskerville

CONTENTS

DINNER LADIES DON'T COUNT

ONE

Jason Paris stormed along Sutton Street. He pulled a fierce face at three girls strung across the pavement and turned left into the school playground. Inside, he kicked every plank in the fence and threw a stone at the huge rubbish bin. It clanged a warning to everyone. Jason had come to school with a smack instead of breakfast and they were all likely to feel the sting.

He barged backwards into the classroom. Miss Smith stopped

smiling at Donna Paget's birthday
cards. There they were, all love and
kisses in her hands – but there was
Jason knocking into chairs.
There was a time and a
place for everything,
and she had to stop
someone getting hurt.

'Hello, Jason. Do you want to use
the plasticine this morning?' she

asked. Miss Smith knew the look, knew the sound of trouble.

'No!' Jason dug his hands into his pockets and glared at anyone foolish enough to look at him.

Donna Paget scooped up her birthday cards and pushed them hurriedly into her tray. 'He spoils everything,' she said.

'Would you like to read a book?' Miss Smith was asking.

Growling something in his throat, Jason cut a path through chairs and children to the book corner. He kicked a cushion and threw himself to the floor with a book. He could smell the dust in the hard, thin carpet. He felt the rough ridges beneath his elbows. It was a cheat, the book corner, he thought. It looked nice, but the floor and the books were too hard. He'd like to throw the books all round the room.

The book he had was big and flat and had sharp corners. It would be a good weapon. He stared at the shiny cover. All about dogs. Dogs! It would be about dogs! He twisted it in his hands like a bar bender in a circus,

hoping it would bend and crack. But it was tougher than he was. Red in the face, he had to give up.

He stared at the poodle on the cover and he thought about his dog, Digger. Digger, small and tough, that got through little  cracks and came back with bones. Digger, that let only him put his lead on, that trotted by his side and looked up when he talked to him. Digger, that waited for him while he did things,

that barked at people he wanted to frighten, and bit people he wanted bitten. That was his dog, Digger.

Poor Digger. Jason's stomach rolled with an empty feeling of loss. He felt sad – and to think that on top of that he'd had a hard smack, just for making a fuss about it!

Miss Smith didn't bother Jason with Maths but it was a lot of cutting out paper shapes: squares, triangles and circles. The gummed colours were stuck into Maths books, and the

bits left over went into the bin.
Everyone else was doing it.

With one half-closed eye Jason
watched the activity, all the moving
about for fresh colours, all the trips
to the bin with the scraps. He
watched and he waited until Donna
Paget was up at the desk, part of a
soft wall of good girls, hiding him
from view.

TWO

Donna's plasticine model of the Red Pirate was on a piece of board standing on the window sill. It wasn't far away. It took only a few seconds to walk over to it and press it down flat with the book about dogs. Jason pulled the book off with a tacky jerk and slid back to the book corner. Served her right for showing off about her birthday, he thought. Now the Red Pirate was a red dwarf. And serve the book right too. The stupid poodle deserved to have plasticine on it.

Jason waited: and just as if he'd lit a fuse it was only a few moments before the explosion. Tears and shouts littered the room like the paper. Everyone was sent to their places while Miss Smith stood over the squashed model. Donna sobbed, blotchy and red, while the girls on her table crowded to comfort her.

'What a terrible thing for anyone to do! This was no accident. Some little hooligan has done this!' Miss Smith said.

'If you cry on your birthday you cry all the year,' said Jason.

Miss Smith looked at him. 'Jason Paris, let me see your hands.' She

was over to him in the two strides it
had taken him to get to the model.
He put them out, grubby, but free
from plasticine. He had thrown the
book down to give them to her,
though, and the wrong side had
landed up.

'Worse than I thought!' Miss
Smith said. 'You've ruined a good
book to do it!' She was really angry.
The room went silent. Donna's
tears had dried, her eyes had
narrowed. Everyone was waiting to
see what would happen next.
Squares, triangles and circles
gummed themselves to the wrong

places while they held their breath
and watched.

'You're a nasty, naughty, little
boy, and none of us wants you in our
room, do we, children?'

'No!' they chorused, looking at
one another with good faces.

But suddenly Miss Smith seemed
to turn into someone else. She
crouched down to Jason's level and

held him by the shoulders. 'Oh, Jason! Why, love?' she asked softly.

No one heard any answer. Donna started crying again and the rest chattered in their mixed-up disappointment. It looked as if he wasn't going to be put out of the classroom, or taken to Mrs Cheff, after all.

It was left there, in the air. Mr Lee, the caretaker, came in to change the roller towel and he saw the overflowing bin. He tut-tutted at the mess and took it out to empty: and that filled the last few minutes before play.

During play-time they talked, Jason and Miss Smith. She drove the

others out and took him to her chair,
where she spoke in a quiet voice and
tried to look him in the eye.

'You came in this morning like
a bear with a sore head,' she said.
'Did you get out of the wrong side of
the bed?'

Jason frowned. When your bed
was against the wall there was only
one side you could get out. And what
did getting out of bed have to do
with any stupid bear? He didn't see

what she was getting at. It was his
dog, Digger, he'd been thinking
about when he got out of bed.

'You think about it while I run
and get my tea,' Miss Smith said.
But it didn't get them anywhere.
When she got back, Jason could still
only stare silently at the floor.

They were frozen like that, in
failure, when the others came in
from play. 'You'd better sit down,
Jason,' Miss Smith said, 'and be nice
and good for the rest of the day.'

Jason didn't know whether he would or not. He didn't feel like being bad any more, and yet he didn't feel like being good. But he definitely wasn't ready to be *nice*. Just to be left to himself to get over Digger seemed about right for him.

'Come on, it's time for P.E. in the

hall. A run round will do you good.'

He had just got his shorts from his tray when a new shriek from Donna made every back in the room go rigid.

THREE

'They're gone!' she screamed, staring with bolt eyes at Miss Smith. Her fists were clenched and her pink arms were shaking. 'My birthday cards! Out of my tray!'

Her tray was on the table. Already, friendly hands were searching in it, checking in case the cards were in her books: and while the shrieking went on the undressed room looked in the other trays, in vases, in the fish tank, even.

But Miss Smith was looking in just

one place – at Jason. Slowly, she crooked her finger and drew him to her. He went, willing and innocent. After all, he hadn't taken Donna's cards, had he?

'I'm going to give you just ten seconds to tell me where they are. I tried to help you. I trusted you. I left you on your own while I went to get my tea, and you repaid me by doing something stupid with Donna's cards. Now, where are they, before I get really cross?'

'I don't know, Miss. Honest!'

'One, two, three, four ... You're a very unkind boy. Five. I don't like people who *won't* be helped. Six, seven, eight, nine, ten.'

She seemed to speed up at the

end. There was no nine-and-a-half, no nine-and-three-quarters this time. She wasn't bluffing. She was ready to do what she'd threatened before.

'Come on, to Mrs Cheff. And the rest of you get changed back. We've missed our hall time now, thanks to one of us . . .'

Miss Smith led Jason by the wrist along the corridor to the head's office.

Mrs Cheff's door was open. Jason could see her in there, getting the birthday log ready with the candles on it. A birthday badge lay like a medal on the table. It would be his turn next week, but he didn't want it to come any more.

Soon Mrs Cheff had him on her own. 'Well, Jason, this is all very disappointing. Now what would possess you to do a thing like this? Why are you in such an ill humour?'

Jason looked at Mrs Cheff's shoes. He wasn't ill, or funny or anything. Everything would be all right if he hadn't had the bad news about his dog, Digger.

And he no more wanted to touch Donna Paget's cards than he wanted one of those birthday badges for himself next week.

There was a knock at Mrs Cheff's door. She had a lot to do.

'Well, I'm going to give you till the end of dinner-time to find them,' she said. 'Or I'm going to have to write a letter home. You can look through the book corner and see if they haven't got tucked inside a book . . .' She gave him a knowing look. She knew where boys hid

things like other people's birthday
cards, it said.

Mr Lee came in with some letters.
He slid them round the door so as
not to disturb her. Mr Lee had a
tattoo on his arm which Jason
admired: a tiger's head with bared
fangs. Jason always looked for it.

Suddenly, seeing it now, he
remembered that he'd seen it once
before that morning. Yes! When Mr
Lee had emptied the bin of paper ...
Now he knew where to look for
those cards. He didn't understand

what Miss Smith and Mrs Cheff
went on about half the time; but now
he did know how he could stop
himself getting another smack at
home.

FOUR

The huge rubbish bin was chained to the fence in the playground. Every Monday morning the rubbish lorry came and picked it up like some robot drinking from a giant mug. You could get up on the bin, if you used the chains for your feet, and then you could look down inside. It was very dangerous, and against the school rules. On the other hand, Jason knew where the birthday cards were – and at dinner time there were only dinner ladies on duty.

As soon as the rest went into the kitchen he ran to the bin. He jumped for the chain and started hauling himself up the cold, smooth side.

'Here, you're not supposed to go up there,' a big girl told him.

'Don't care. Mind your own business.'

'Mrs Moors can see you.'

'Clear off!' he reached for the rim.

'She's a dinner lady. You'll get into trouble.'

'Dinner ladies don't count,' he
said, and he heaved himself on to the
flat top. Now all he had to do was
take the small lid off and look down
inside. Being Friday, this morning's
rubbish shouldn't be hard to reach.

But Mrs Moors came quicker than
the lid came away in his hand.

'Jason, get down from up there,'
she said. 'You'll fall down inside.'

He didn't reply. He tugged at the
rubbery lid, and at last it came
away, heavy in his hand.

'I said, come down!'

'I'm looking for something.'

'What are you looking for?'

'Something.'

He didn't like the smell coming up; and it was darker in there than he'd thought. But the real trouble was, he couldn't reach the top layer of rubbish, not without climbing in. He looked down outside for Mrs Moors again: could he get in before she stopped him? But she wasn't where she had been, beside the bin. She was coming across the playground, carrying a pair of steps.

If she was coming up to drag him down he'd have to get in quick!

'You get in there and I'll kill you!' she shouted. 'Never mind what Mrs Cheff says.'

It stopped Jason dead.

'Now let's see what you're so blessed worked up about. A ball, is it?' Mrs Moors was up the steps and reaching down into the bin. She scooped up handfuls of coloured paper. 'No ball in here,' she said.

'It's birthday cards. Someone's thrown out Donna Paget's birthday cards, and I've got the blame.'

Mrs Moors went on scooping. 'Well, you can't blame them for that,' she said. 'You've had the hump all day, haven't you? I saw you pass my window this morning, all in your temper.' She took out

grabs of paper and let them drift
back down. 'There's no cards in
here, Jason.' She put the lid back.
'Now, you come down and tell me
what's given you the hump.'

Jason came down. He liked this
dinner lady. He understood her. She
seemed to talk the same way as he
did. Yes, he'd had the hump all
right, been in his temper. But it
wasn't his fault, was it, after what
had happened?

FIVE

He told her, there behind the bin.
He thought she'd understand.

'It's my dog,' he said. 'Digger.
He's not really a dog yet, he's one
I was going to have next week. For
my birthday. My mum promised me
years ago. But now she says she's
made ill by dog's fur, and I can't
have one.' He kicked the fence
again, remembering.

'Oh.' Mrs Moors seemed lost for
a word. 'Allergic,' she said, after
a few seconds. 'Gets up her nose,
I suppose.'

'Yeah, and she gets up mine!'

Mrs Moors laughed, and ruffled his hair. 'Oh, come on, she has a lot to put up with, your mum. She's probably thinking it wouldn't be fair to the dog, her out to work all day, the dog cooped up.'

Jason kicked the fence again.

'Hard old life, isn't it, Jason? I wish I had a dog you could walk for me – but I haven't. You've just got to swallow it, wait till your mum's ready. It'll happen one day, you see . . .'

Jason shrugged. Who knew when that would ever be? And in the meantime he was still in trouble over Donna Paget's birthday cards. 'The

cards,' he said. 'I know I never went near them.'

'Well, they're not in the bin, so they're somewhere in your classroom,' Mrs Moors said. 'Come on, let's turn it upside down.'

Miss Smith was in the classroom, carefully stretching the Red Pirate to something like his right size. Mrs Moors went over to her and they had a very quiet conversation. Jason knew what it was about. Mrs Moors was telling Miss Smith about his birthday, and Digger.

While they talked Jason thought back to that morning. In his mind he came into the classroom again, and he tried to see what he'd seen before. He saw Donna Paget grabbing up her cards and pushing them into her tray. She'd done it all in a rush, as if he was going to tear them up.

Jason went over to the tray unit. Donna's tray was at the top, with her name on it. He pulled it out. As usual on P.E. days, it was stuffed full with plimsolls and a tee-shirt.

It was chock-a-block, like his own untidy drawers at home.

And then he knew where to look: where he sometimes found things if he turned his own room upside down, like Mrs Moors had said. Where his football programmes went if he over-stuffed his drawers. Down the back, where top things slid if you pulled the drawer in and out carelessly.

Sure enough, there they were: all the cards, chewed and bent at the back.

'Look!' he said. But he didn't touch them. He didn't want anyone to think he'd put them back.

'Oh, lovely. Well done, Jason. How clever! You see?'

The two women were beaming: and inside Jason felt pleased.

Miss Smith turned to Mrs Moors. 'I was mistaken,' she said. 'Because he was naughty once I blamed him twice. Give a dog a bad name!'

Jason frowned. Now he didn't understand again. Was she talking about him? She had to be, he thought, because Digger was a *good* name to give a dog.

And one day he'd give a dog that name; when the time came . . .

LINDA'S LIE

Author's note:

When paper money buys less and less and gets passed about so often that it tears, it has to be changed for hard-wearing coins.

This book was first made at the awkward time when the old pound notes were about to be replaced by new pound pieces. It gave us a problem, but in the end we decided that the important pound in the story should be a coin – even though it might seem strange to the first readers.

After all, we didn't want the book to 'wear out' as quickly as paper money does!

B.A.

ONE

'What's that school playing at? Don't they know there's no pound pieces here to spare for *outings*?' Mr Steel said the word as if it tasted bad in his mouth.

Linda looked up at his stern, black face, at the eyes which were telling a different story to the mouth. Her father smacked his knee with the flat of his hand. She knew that sign. He was just as angry with himself for not having the money to spare.

But still she said it. She wanted

him to know all the facts before they
threw a cover over the whole idea,
like putting the yellow canary to
sleep for the night. 'It's the ballet,'
she said. '*The Sleeping Beauty* in a
theatre. That's why it's a pound.'

'I'll do you a dance for sixpence,
girl.' He smiled: but once more his
eyes and his mouth were at odds.

'The letter says see Miss if it's
hardship over money ...'

She thought his head was going to hit the ceiling. 'Hardship over money? *Hardship over money?* Sweet Lord, I'll give your Miss "hardship over money"! Does she know there's no money to go looking for work some mornings? Does she know your brother needs new shoes, your mattress can't be fit for a dog to lie on, your mam and me's fed up to kingdom come with the taste of jam – and she wants to take you to the ballet! Hardship over money is right – but you don't catch me asking favours for that my girl. That don't come into it, no way!'

He pushed out of the door and thumped up the stairs to the bathroom – while the canary screeched in fright and seed went flying all over.

Linda climbed on to a chair and pulled the cover over the bird. 'There!' she said. 'Now shut up – 'cos that's that!' And on flat feet she went to find her mam, all that walking on her toes forgotten.

TWO

Linda didn't really know how to tell
Miss Smith. She knew her teacher
wanted all of them to go, and she
knew the school had money for the
ones who couldn't afford it. Which
meant Miss Smith would be upset if
Linda's parents didn't want to ask
for it.

'Don't you *want* to go, Linda?'
she'd ask. 'I always thought you
were so keen.' How could she tell her
that her daddy didn't think it was
important? That would be like

saying something against Miss Smith.

The other trouble was, it was always done in the open – all in the classroom where the others could hear. Wouldn't Donna Paget make a meal of it? A fuss like that. And Jason Paris? He could squash you down with something he said as easy as he squashed other people's plasticine.

No. She'd have to find some other excuse. She was going to have to tell Miss Smith a lie.

In the classroom Monday morning all the money was starting to come in. There were pounds here and pounds there, some held out on palms like sports day medals and

others clutched tight like family
jewels. Even Jason Paris had his,
a handful of heavy silver in tens,
clunking on the table top.

Linda's name came half-way
down the girls. Most times people
were getting noisy by then – but
today they were as quiet as mice.

'Linda Steel?'

'Please, Miss, I'm not going,
Miss.' Linda felt bad already, and
she was only telling the truth so far.

Miss Smith looked up at her, surprised. Across the other side Donna Paget coughed, or something.

'You're not going, Linda? Oh dear. Why ever not?' For a second or two she sat waiting for the reason: then she must have guessed it could be awkward. 'Come up here, love.'

Linda went out to the front. Everyone stared. It was still so quiet she felt like a dancer about to do one of the hard bits.

'Please, Miss,' Linda said, stopping and taking a deep breath, getting close enough to smell the teacher's hair. 'I've got to go to a christening.'

'Really? On a Monday?'

'I think it's special,' she said in a
low voice. She looked at Miss Smith.
She was nodding.

Lying was easier than she thought.
All you had to do was say it.

'Well, they can't change
that, I suppose. And we can't
change the day, either.
What a shame – and you're
one of my best dancers.'

Linda smiled a brave, sad smile
which said all she needed. A lie
smile. That was easy, too.

'What church is that, then?'
Donna Paget asked at playtime.
Donna had very good ears, Linda
thought – or else she could *see* what
people said.

'Somewhere up London. A special

one. They have their Sundays on
Mondays.'

'That's silly. Never heard of that
before.'

'Well, you have now, haven't
you?'

'Who's it being christened?'

'My uncle,' Linda said. She didn't
know what made her say it, what
made the lie get bigger. But she had
heard of grown-ups having it done –
and this day did have to be a bit
special.

Donna Paget crossed her legs the

way her mother did when she busted
her sides. 'They'll have a job lifting
him up for the water bit,' she
laughed.

Linda stared her out. 'He's not
very heavy,' she answered.

But she knew that was wrong.
The whole thing was going wrong
already – and she'd only just started
the lie.

THREE

Mr Steel came away from the window and crackled the envelope in his fingers. He walked past the end of the out-of-work line and found a hard bench to sit on. Carefully, he opened what he had in his hand. When he hadn't earned it, it hardly seemed his to touch, let alone his to risk tearing. But he counted it, the notes and the jangle of coins which came last.

He sighed. There was a use for it all, and none left over. Shaking his head, he turned up his collar and went out. It was a long walk home when you had to pretend the buses weren't going your way.

But the buses going past weren't passing just him. With all the rest of the traffic they were skimming past a stranded car at the side of the road. The car rocked with the buffeting of air, and the man who was bent over by the wheel was swearing.

'Blessed garages!' he said, throwing the wheel-brace into the kerb. 'They don't think someone might have to undo these blessed nuts!'

Mr Steel stopped. He knew the problem. Garages put the wheel-nuts on with special tools, and getting

them off when you had a puncture
was murder.

'Stupid little wheel-brace!' the
man was saying. 'It's got no *push*.'

The man was in a suit, but his
hands and face were grimy with car
dirt.

Mr Steel stopped. 'Let's have a go,
mate. See if a fresh pair of hands can
do it.'

The man looked hard at Mr Steel
and picked up the wheel-brace.
'Thanks a lot,' he said.

Mr Steel took a firm grip and
pulled, and pushed. But he couldn't
shift any of the nuts on his own.

'Give it a go together,' he said,
rubbing his hands and drawing
breath.

They had to hug to do it. Hands just fitting side by side on the wheel-brace, arms round each other's waists. Cheek to cheek, black and white, breathing in each other's breath, they one-two-three'd, and strained, and arched . . . and shifted the first nut. And then the other three.

'Phew! Thanks a lot, mate. I'm

very grateful to you.' He pushed an oily hand into his pocket and pulled out a pound piece. 'You'll have a drink with me, won't you?'

Mr Steel looked at the man. Don't spoil it by offering me money, his eyes seemed to say. And then they seemed to think of something else.

'All right, friend, I will.' He took the coin. 'Good health,' he said.

'Cheers,' said the man. 'You saw me out of trouble, there.'

FOUR

At home, the last thing Linda
wanted was any talk of ballet, or
dancing, or theatres. Even school
seemed a dangerous subject to get
on. She didn't want her father
angry about the outing, or sorry. She
didn't want her mother taking her
side or her brother Michael asking
questions. She had started something
off – something bad – and all she
wanted now was for next Monday to
come and go with nothing said.

She'd have liked to hibernate till

Tuesday. But she couldn't do that. She had to stew inside, and act normal.

That evening she sat in front of the television in dread of *Blue Peter* doing a bit about the ballet. Or of Michael kicking his leg over the chair arm and asking whose room she'd go in when her class was out. She didn't want him looking for her in school that day.

What did you do out of school all

day anyway? Someone could see you
– even your father, when he was out
looking for work!

Her heart turned over when he
came in. It was horrible. She wasn't
pleased to see him. She had to act it.
Is this what being a liar's like? she
thought. This nasty pain all the time,
and not being able to look straight at
your dad?

And he seemed all full of himself
today – taller in the doorway. But he
didn't say why, not to her, nor to
Michael. He looked at the TV set,
hummed a little something deep in
his throat and went out to the
kitchen.

It was bed-time before Linda
found out what it was. And then it

wasn't her father who told her. He wasn't a showy man.

'Look!' said her mother as she tucked Linda in on the lumpy mattress. She held out a shiny pound piece. 'This is for your outing. Your daddy got it extra today. Did a little job for a man he met. We won't miss it, being extra.' She was smiling such a happy smile.

Linda looked up at the coin. It should have looked good and made

her smile, but it didn't. It looked like money from another country. Even the Queen looked cross as if she was saying, 'We've found you out, Linda Ann Steel. Look where lying leads you . . .'

Linda's eyes filled with tears. She put her head under the blankets to hide them – and she suddenly felt like their silent canary must feel covered, and trapped: only she was in a cage of lies.

'Ah – don't cry, Petal.' Her mother patted the mound of her head. 'It's a happy ending to the story, eh?'

FIVE

The cold coin in Linda's sock seemed to stick out like some nasty bite. You could see it if you knew where to look for it, even with white socks on. And you'd see where it had been when she took them off for dance, grazing her all grey where it scratched her ankle.

But she didn't know what else to do with it. She couldn't just give it in and say she was going to the ballet after all. Not really. They didn't cancel christenings just like that, and

she'd made it sound much too
important to just have changed her
mind.

There was nowhere to hide it
at home where someone wouldn't
come across it – and nobody's place
was secret enough in school. The
only other thing would be to throw
it away. But she shivered at the
thought. A picture in her head of her
father working for it made the
money much too precious for that.

It weighed her down as if it had
been in pennies. Why had she had to
tell Miss Smith a lie? It had seemed
easy at first, but now it was getting
harder and harder every minute.

With her bag held against her leg
she went into the classroom. Today

she really didn't want to be at school. But if she thought things were bad there was worse to come. Life could play some terrible tricks.

'Listen, children, I've got something important to ask you. Andrew Field has lost his ballet money. He thinks he left it in his bag in the cloakroom – silly boy – but he's just been back to look, and it isn't there.'

Everyone looked at Andrew Field, mouths in little O's. He put on a tragic face and stared at his *Happy Reader*. Then they looked for Jason Paris: but he was late again. He'd kick his way into the classroom in a minute – in a mood, but innocent!

'Mind you, Andrew could have dropped it somewhere else. So if anyone comes across it I'll be very grateful.'

Linda remembered past fusses about missing things. A feeling of nobody being trusted would hang in the classroom till the money was found, or it was forgotten.

'Anyway, it's our hall time now, so let's get changed for it quickly and quietly.'

Now Linda had to take her socks off. And just as she knew it would, the pound piece in the right one seemed to burn like something jumped out from a bonfire. If anyone saw that now it would be much too late to say she'd brought her money to go after all. There'd be all sorts of questions asked, and Donna Paget would think it was Christmas. They'd have to talk to her parents to clear it up, and then all the christening lie would come out.

'Hurry up, Linda. Come on, it's not like you to be slow for dance.'

But getting off a sock with money in it was every bit as difficult as Linda thought it would be. The hard-edged lump kept riding up with her leg and seemed to want to jump itself out and on to the floor. And trapping it between her thumb and her sock only left that guilty secret showing in her hand.

There was only one last chance. She pretended the sock was too tight and did the other one instead. If she hid the money leg, she told herself, she could do it while the others went out of the room.

She pulled her dress over her head, folded it with the one sock

hidden, and sat up straight with her arms on the desk. Ready. The whole room was ready.

'Good.' Miss Smith stood up.

'Please, Miss, Linda Steel's left one sock on!' Donna Paget sounded as if she'd discovered a new planet. And everyone laughed as if it was the best joke ever invented. Even Andrew Field forgot he was supposed to be worried sick about his money.

Linda closed her eyes. Tight, dry, guilty eyes.

'Come on,' said Miss Smith.

'Silly girl. Clocks won't stop for you.' She hurried in a zig-zag between the tables. 'Cock your leg up.'

There was nothing else Linda

could do. She was done for. Inside she had that empty, helpless feeling of just going off under gas at the dentist's. She felt Miss Smith lift her foot, and she thought she heard her own voice saying something beginning with 'I . . .' She could hear the class laughing at the sight of Miss Smith helping her. But no noise was loud enough to cover the sound of the pound as its hard, ringing edge hit the floor.

'Whee, Miss . . .'

'Linda Steel!'

'Hey, look, Andrew . . .'

Public shock. Private glee. Even good friends drew in their breath.

'I think you'd better take this

money and have a little talk with
Mrs Cheff, Linda,' said Miss Smith.
'Don't you?'

SIX

It was a cold and windy morning but
Mr Steel forced himself to be up and
out at his old time for work. It did no
good to let things slide. Besides, there
was something special he had to do
before he could rest easy in his mind.

He went to the end of the street
and pulled himself into the telephone
box. In a few moments – using the
phone as an ear-muff against the
icy blast coming through a broken
pane – he was talking to Linda's
headmistress.

'It's a jolly good job you phoned,' Mrs Cheff told him after hearing what he wanted. 'Linda's not down as going, not on the list. She said something about going to a christening.'

Mr Steel frowned. It was a bad line and the cold wind was howling. It had almost sounded like *christening*, what the headmistress had said. 'No, it's the dancing she wants. I give her the money, only it was late and I was scared the seats had all run out.'

'Really, they get so muddled!' Mrs Cheff complained. 'And they seem to think money grows on trees, don't they?'

Mr Steel didn't answer. That bit didn't sound like Linda.

'I'll find out why she hasn't paid.
I'm sure we've still got a seat. I just
hope she hasn't lost the money.'

'So do I,' said Mr Steel. 'So do I.'
And shaking his head he put the
phone back on its cold cradle.

SEVEN

Mrs Cheff took Linda into her room. She sat in her swivel chair and looked at the red-eyed girl. 'Really, Linda! You do seem to have lost your senses. How could you be so stupid with someone else's money?'

Linda's toes curled into the flattened carpet. She frowned at Mrs Cheff's knees. Everything had got out of hand so quickly. She didn't know what to do, what to say. If she told Mrs Cheff the truth, what would her father say about the lie? But, then, what would he say about them thinking she'd stolen somebody's pound?

'It's just as well the pound turned up, isn't it?'

Linda stared at Mrs Cheff. But she kept her mouth shut tight. How did she know about the money down her sock? Miss Smith hadn't told her – she'd left that to Linda. Could she see through the wall or something, like she always said she could?

'Your father phoned – sensible man – so I knew you had a pound to pay. No thanks to you, Linda, was it?'

Linda shook her head. He'd phoned? Then Mrs Cheff knew she was supposed to go. That meant she knew she wasn't a thief. But it also meant she'd found out about the lie!

'Although I still don't know why you said you were going to a christening. Your father didn't seem to understand either. Unless it was something to do with what we're going to see. *The Sleeping Beauty*. Was it some silly joke about seeing the baby's christening on the stage?'

It went very quiet in the small room. Linda heard the sounds of music from the hall and wished she

were there with the rest of the class.
She looked at her feet. So Mrs Cheff
thought she'd said something clever
about the ballet to Miss Smith –
a joke, not a lie.

She wanted to nod. She could
easily nod and keep quiet, she
thought. Nothing needed to be said.

That would leave the whole thing
sorted out.

But Mrs Cheff didn't give her time
to work out what to do. 'What I
don't understand most of all, though,
is how you could think a whole
pound piece was so *unimportant*.
Fancy not telling us about it! A

pound was a pound in my day, you know.'

What was that? *Unimportant*? Linda's stare was sore, and shocked. Mrs Cheff could say what she liked about stealing or lying – but no one in her house thought a pound piece was *unimportant*! She knew the worth of a pound better than Mrs Cheff did. And that pound had been worth ten to her father. For his sake she couldn't keep quiet about that.

'I wasn't being stupid with that money, Miss. I was *hiding* it. I didn't drop it down a drain, did I?'

'Didn't drop it down a drain?'

But now Linda was crying, and
telling it all. In a thin, sobbing voice
she was pouring out the whole story:
all about her not going to the ballet
at first, and the reason; and the lie to
Miss Smith; and the mix-up over
Andrew Field's money, and
the pound down her sock.

At the end she took a deep breath
and thrust out her hand with the hot
pound in it.

Mrs Cheff looked hard at it, and
swivelled to pick up another pound
piece from her desk. She frowned,
then her face seemed to clear.

'I *see*,' she said. 'Then this isn't
yours at all. It's Andrew Field's.
I found it after your father phoned,
in the cloakroom – rolled behind

the door. He's the careless one.
This is the money I was on about.'

Linda's shoulders heaved in
another sob. But it was the last. It
had been good to clear everything
up.

'Well, thank you for telling me,
Linda.' She gave her arm a squeeze.
'I'm very glad you did. It was
important, wasn't it?' She gave her a
pat on the head. 'Now you'd better
get back to lessons. You're missing
your chance to dance.'

Linda couldn't trust herself to say
thank you. She hurried out to find

the others in the hall, her eyes still red, but with a new, smooth feeling inside.

Miss Smith must have told them to say no more, because no one even looked at her. She stood in the doorway, listening. The music was beautiful, the sort that lifted the heart.

She glided into it with a lightness and a joy that only she could know about – like a happy bird with the cover off, suddenly released to dance free in the sky.